THE
SIXTY
SECONDS

THE SIXTY SECONDS

ALAN R. OWENS

The Sixty Seconds

Copyright © 2019 by Alan R. Owens. All rights reserved.

No part of this publication may be reproduced, stored in a retrieval system or transmitted in any way by any means, electronic, mechanical, photocopy, recording or otherwise without the prior permission of the author except as provided by USA copyright law.

This is a work of fiction. Names, descriptions, entities, and incidents included in the story are products of the author's imagination. Any resemblance to actual persons, events, and entities is entirely coincidental.

The opinions expressed by the author are not necessarily those of URLink Print and Media.

1603 Capitol Ave., Suite 310 Cheyenne, Wyoming USA 82001
1-888-980-6523 | admin@urlinkpublishing.com

URLink Print and Media is committed to excellence in the publishing industry.

Book design copyright © 2019 by URLink Print and Media. All rights reserved.

Published in the United States of America
ISBN 978-1-64367-823-8 (Paperback)
ISBN 978-1-64367-822-1 (Digital)

15.08.19

Chapter 1

It all started the day Jason fell victim to the juggernaut that corporations were euphemizing as "downsizing." He had been employed the National Integrated System Software Corporation, commonly known as NISS, in Denver for 25 years as a software engineer and fully intended with the same until retirement. He was proud of the job he had done and felt that the company had, in turn, been loyal to him. In retrospect Jason could now blame only himself for his naivte—if not just plain stupidity. There was no longer any such thing as loyalty—at least on the part of a company. An employee was loyal was, if not a complete fool, then at least hopelessly short-sighted. The signs of the time were evident for anyone with eyes opened. The problem was that Jason had essentially been keeping his eyes closed—his head in the sand in good ostrich fashion. He had relied on the fact that he was doing, and had always done a good job—putting in many extra unpaid hours to ensure that his work was top notch. It was almost in a state of shock that Jason packed up his personal belongings and hauled them out to his aging BMW. As he pulled down the picture of Katy, his wife and his two sons, Jeff and Jim, he felt that he had somehow let them down. There were certificates of achievement and excellence and Jason simply threw these in his trash can. Several papers needed to be signed—then Jason turned in his badge and was finished. He walked out the security gate for the last time and wondered what the future held. Some of his colleagues had been updating their resumes and arranging interviews at other software companies but they had had little or no success as there appeared to be a glut of software engineers n the Denver area. Jason had not even bothered to make up a resume—such had been his confidence.

As Jason pulled out of the parking lot onto the busy 50 mph boulevard his thoughts were far removed from his driving. Too late he glanced in his rear-view mirror and saw the ten-wheeler bearing down on him at an alarming rate. The vehicle immediately filled the rear-view mirror and then there was the sound of screeching brakes. Jason felt the impact of the collision and an instant of searing pain. Then the pain ceased and he found himself back in the line of cars waiting to turn onto the boulevard. He found himself shaking and sweating and a car behind him honked—another angry laid-off engineer wanting to escape the scene. The car in front of him had moved up so Jason inched forward and then pulled up on the grassy median that separated incoming and outgoing traffic. He then rested his head on the steering wheel and waited for the shaking to subside. He was confused and helpless and needed time to try and figure out what had just happened. He knew that he had been hit by the semi—that much he remembered. How then had he ended up back on the parking lot exit road and not having yet turned onto the boulevard?

His mind refused to function and then Jason decided that this was neither the time nor the place to figure things out. He sat in his vehicle for a few minutes and then a polite driver let him get back into the line and he did so. This time he exited with more card and saw the semi roll by that had certainly killed hm a minute earlier. Jason needed a drink and a place to sit down and ponder the matter. He passed Smitty's, a local watering hoe for NISS employees, but noticed that the parking lot was full. The establishment was certain to be filled with former NISS programmers crying on each other's shoulders. Deciding that this wasn't what he needed at the time, Jason drove on until he reached a small bar that he had frequented on several occasions. He parked and entered, finding that he was the only customer at that early hour. He replied somewhat shortly to the bartender's "good afternoon" and ordered a double Vodka Collins. In the corner stood a cigarette machine and Jason couldn't help himself despite having quit smoking four months earlier. He asked the bartender for change and purchased a pack. He thought about something light but finally reverted to his old standby—Kook Filter Kings. A moment later Jason had a smoking cigarette in one hand and a drink in the other.

    He was torn between thinking about the loss of his job and the singular incident with the truck. He decided that he had to understand the truck incident before he could even consider anything else. What exactly had happened? The facts were simple enough. He had pulled out into the patch of an oncoming ten-wheeler and given the driver no chance whatsoever to avoid the collision. The crash had seemed to take place but then conditions had changed to those immediately preceding the turn that had precipitated the collision in the first place. The only explanation that Jason could come up with was that he had somehow imagined the whole thing—even the concussion of the impact as well as the instant of intense pain. Perhaps the shock of losing his job had something to do with it. Feeling at least semi-satisfied with his conclusion, Jason finished his drink and began to stand up to leave. Suddenly he found himself sitting again with the glass still one-third full—the third he had just swallowed or so he had thought. Jason shook is head, finished the drink for the send time, and walked out of the bar.

Chapter 2

As Jason drove the 20 miles to his suburban home in Thornton his mind was in a state of turmoil. He knew he would have to find a job as quickly as possible and that was easier said that done. He was fully aware of the fact that those associates of his who had searched for new jobs had been unsuccessful. A job search now would be even more difficult due to the fact that over a hundred newly released NISS programmers would also be in the market. This would simply add to the glut of programmers. Jason wished now that he had trained in some sort of a backup profession such as plumbing or as an electrician—anything that was at all practical. This was something he had tried to impress upon his sons but to no avail. Jim was enrolled in college at the University of Rochester and majoring in chemical engineering. Jeff was still in high school but showed no interest in attending a trade school for two years before entering college.

Despite the torrent of thoughts in Jason's head, he drove with awareness and care due to the scare he had so recently received. He dreaded facing is wife, Katy. She was working now but would be home in several hours. She worked at St. Joseph's hospital as a nurse. Jason thought about calling her but decided the bad news could wait a little longer while he tried to compose himself somewhat. Also, we would have to apprise Jeff of the news when he got home from school. Jim also needed to be called but that could wait a few days.

Perhaps the worst problem that Jason faced was the Bricker financial situation. Due to various factors they were quite deeply in debt. One element was the money they had spent on the boys.

Since childhood the latter had not lacked for anything—including transformers and GI Joe and their various "rides—whatever the vogue at the time happened to be. They had both attended private schools where tuition, once the reached high school age, rivaled that of most colleges. Jim had initially had a full scholarship to the University of Rochester but, due to some university politics, lost it. Both boys drove newer cars than Jason or Katy.

At one time NISS had been generous with severance pay but not this time. Jason could count on only 2 weeks pay as could all those who had been laid off—regardless of time of service. In times past the policy had been one week of severance pay per year of service which would have given Jason some 6 months to find a job. There had been talk among the laid-off employees that morning of trying to sue the company because of the change of severance pay policy. Jason doubted, however, that anything would come of such a suit as he had never seen anything in print to the effect that the company was obligated to make any severance payments whatsoever. Some of the older employees told him that he was correct and that the company had simply chosen to abide by the one week per service year convention I the past. Now that its very survival was threatened all bets were off.

Finally, Jason turned into his driveway and was relieved to note that neither Katy's nor Jeff's vehicles was present. It was so hot that he put on a pair of shorts along with a 9th Infantry Vietnam T-shirt. Yes, he had fought for his country but that didn't matter now. The next thing he did was to mix a Vodka Collins and sit down to think things out. Under the conditions we he would have to.

exercise caution or Mr. Vodka would get the upper hand. Jason had already been through periods where drinking had taken over much of his life. The also lit a Kool although he intended to quit shortly but the again….

Next Jason lay on a recliner in the shade and mentally revisited the incident at the plant where he seemed to have been hit by the truck. How could he have so vividly imagined such an occurrence? His only explanation was the one he had come up with at the bar—it must have been just a matter or stress and nothing more. Everyone knew that stress can do strange things to people—it can after them in insidious ways. Who knew what some of the other now unemployed programmers were suffering. Perhaps his own problem was minor in comparison.

This brought Jason to thinking more about the bar. Was this just a matter of forgetfulness or what? He remembered finishing his drink and standing up. Then je had suddenly been sitting again with a drink yet to be finished. Once again Jason could only blame the trauma of the entire morning,

Jason soon found himself on his third Vodka Collins and decided that he'd better do something other than sit and drink. All he needed was for Katy to come home and find him not only jobless but drunk. He decided that his first order of business should be to write a resume–something that he hadn't done for 23 years, He went to his filing cabinet and retrieved a file labeled "Employee Information." The file contained little—his original resume and certificates of promotion. He could recall what the certificates he had thrown away were for. He spread these out his desk and started up his computer. He already knew hot to go about the job of writing a resume because he had not only observed the as his job-seeking coworkers had done theirs, but had actually assisted then at times. He was well aware of the fact that the new trend in resumes was to get everything on a single page. You were to start with your most recent activity and then work backwards. At each step you were to include what you felt you had done for you company. You were to list your job titles, your responsibilities and then how you had fulfilled these responsibilities. Jason dd a search on the until he found a resume format that appeared to him. Within an hour and, with the help of Bill Gate's Microsoft Word, he felt that he had a credible document.

With this chore behind him, Jason felt a little better and mixed another Vodka Collins. He had been in a state of complete concentration and hadn't even thought about the two strange incidents. Next he decided to mow the lawn. He needed something to keep from drinking and dwelling on his unemployment. Jason went out to the garage and drug out his 15-year-old Sears Craftsman mower. As usual it took about 10 tried to get the mower started.

Finally, the engine caught and he began mowing a swath next to the driveway. He was almost to the end of his second swath when it happened. Suddenly he was back in the driveway and attempting to start the mover. The swaths that he had mowed lay uncut.

Jason was shaken, this was the third episode of the day and something strange was indeed happening. It seemed that he was taking little trips back in time. That morning his life had been saved by such a trip, He had indeed been run down by a semi. He estimated that he had gone back about sixty seconds in time on that occasion. The second time around Jason had been able to stop before entering the boulevard and avoid the collision. For that reason only was he still alive. The incident at the bar had been a manifestation of the same phenomenon. He had indeed finished the drink the first time. Then cane the time irregularity and he was left with a third of his drink untouched. Next came the lawn mower incident.

Jason was frightened but also fascinated as the started the lawn mower again. This time he counted the seconds until he got to where he had been interrupted the first time. He calculated that his time displacement had entailed a time frame of about 60 second. He found himself mouthing "sixty-thousand as he reached his previous spot in the second swatch. This would certainly account for the other two episodes. Apparently, anything that happened during that minute was undone after that time had elapsed. It was as if nothing had transpired during that time.

Jason now had a million questions and no answers. What was the cause of these time slips, now whatever one night choose to call them? Were they and would they and would they always be a matter of 5 seconds in duration? Was he somehow unknowingly invoking them? Did he have any control over them? Could he possibly suppress them? Was there any cure at all? Had anyone else suffered something of the sort?

Suddenly Jason had another thought. It might be that time was rolling back on its own. It was with all these thoughts that he continued cutting the grass and he completed the task without further incident. As he pushed the lawn mower toward the garage, he heard a car door slam in the driveway and he knew that either Jeff or Kary was hone, "Hi Dad," said Jeff as he came around the house into the back yard,

"Hi Jeff," responded Jason. "Hold on a minute," he said as he began emptying the lawn mower bag into the garbage can. Th then proceeded to tell Jeff about his day—omitting for the time being the time slips. As he was talking Katy rolled in and Jason found himself in tears as began repeating his report. Katy tried to reassure him but to no avail. She did promise to take over the bill-paying and to help maintain a strict budget. If Jason hadn't found a job within 2 months there would be no alternative for their other son, Jim, except to get a student loan or to drop out of college. Tomorrow Jason would begin calling the human resource departments of possible employers.

Chapter 3

Two weeks later Jason was totally discouraged. He had, more or less, gone through the yellow pages as far as computers and software companies. The standard message he received was that the concerned company was not hiring at that time but that Jason could call back at a later date if he wished. During the third week he finally got an interview with a small software house. It appeared to Jason, based upon what he was told by the interviewer, that he easily met the requirements. He was then told that he was actually "overqualified." Jason objected quite vehemently and asked how it was possible to be overqualified. The interviewer patiently explained that Jason would undoubtedly "jump jobs" as soon as something became available that was commensurate with his skills. Jason's protests to the contrary got him nowhere. He did get an idea of the direction in which software companies were headed. Wherever possible the wanted to fire new college graduates and then train them—knowing they would work very cheaply as they usually had no families to support. Finally, Jason resorted to a "head-hunter' but nothing had happened as the end of three weeks rolled around.

During the third week Jason underwent several time slips but nothing serious happened. While driving to the store one morning he stopped for a red light. When the light changed he proceeded bit suddenly found himself stopped again at the light. With so little knowledge of the phenomenon, Jason had the irrational fear that he might be stuck at the same light forever. The time slips didn't appear to operate in that manner but who was to say about the future? Jason concentrated upon any type of feeling, etc. that ,ogjt presage an impending attack and believed that he was making some progress. As far as his thoughts they were mostly of his current unemployment and the fact that NISS had let him down. Of course, NISS was almost always on his mind. However, it seemed to Jason that the time slips occurred when he concentrated on the letters of the name without elaboration. This was followed by vague sense of unreality -very slight and very transient.

Another episode had occurred at Jason's single job interview. This one was somewhat embarrassing. When he had arrived at the office the secretary had not been at her desk. Jason had sat down and, when she did appear, he approached her desk and announced his presence. The was told to have a seat and the interviewer would be right with him. Finally, she asked him who he was and whom he was there to see. Jason then realized what had happened. The tine in which he introduced himself had slipped and he hadn't been aware of it. In the eyes of the secretary she had come out from the ladies' room or wherever she happened to be and found a stranger sitting in the office. The man had not approached her but had just remained sitting there. This was rather disturbing but no real harm had been done. As far as the interview went, Jason was, of course, told that he was overqualified.

There had been several additional episodes but no one else had been involved except for the occasion when Jason and Katy had gone out to eat with Katy's superior and her husband. They had gibe to ab "all you can eat" Chinese restaurant and Jason had been returning to their table carrying a huge plate of food in one hand and a bowl of soup in the other. He had attempted to set the plate on the table but it was unbalanced and he dumped the entire contents in the lao of Kay's boss. He immediately concentrated on the initials "NISS" and was thrilled to find himself back at the food counters. This time he carried the plate in two hands and went back a second time for the soup. He was extremely careful and was actually laughing this time when he returned with the soup. The other couple asked him what he was laughing about and he could only reply about how funny it would have been if he had dumped the plate on the floor. He added that he was so hungry he would have had to lap up he food like a dog. The couple laughed indulgently and looked at him rather strangely but said nothing. As for Jason, he began to realize that there was an upside to these time shifts. First of all one of these had undoubtedly saved his life. Furthermore, depending upon his timing, he could atone for a mistake—actually atone wasn't the word. He could actually eliminate a mistake entirely—he could make so the mistake never happened.

It was at this time that Jason decided that it was time to confide in Katy. He had no idea of hos to explain what was going on nor could he realistically expect her to believe him anyway. Not that she would necessarily disbelieve him—she just wouldn't understand nor could he expect her to do so. She would attribute the entire matter to some mental problem and, in fact, he still hadn't ruled that out. Mental problem or not, he was stepping back in time. Taking these little time strolls was actually kind of fun at times but who knew what the eventual outcome would be. They could very well prove harmful to his health. Perhaps the time involved would increase. Jason had no desire to live much of his life over again, should he got back far enough—he had little doubt that he would see to it that he was trained as a plumber, electrician or something of the sort. The whole affair was mind-boggling. Was he the only person in the world with this time traveling "skill." It would seem rather presumptuous to make this assertion but Jason had never heard of such a thing before except in time travel movie and books and there was always some kind of machine involved. Also he couldn't imagine a bunch of people running around and setting the world back by 60 seconds simultaneously.

That very night Jason did apprise Katy of the situation. She was understanding but insisted that his imagination was the culprit -that he had somehow been thrown out of whack by the trauma of losing his job. Her logic was reasonable—in fact she was entertaining the same thoughts that had been running through his mind. Jason tried to present his side of the picture but found that he simply had no proof. Katy suggested that he see either a psychologist or a psychiatrist about the matter. He objected at first because of the expense but finally relented.

It was three days until Jason could see the psychiatrist a Dr. Livingston, who came highly recommended by Cay's co-workers as well as a number of doctors with whom she was acquainted. During the three days Jason experienced time slips on two occasions. He was alone both times as Katy was working and Jeff was at school. On both occasions he had been thinking about his former employer, NISS and perhaps concentrating on the initial, "N.I.S.S." He now felt that he could, at least sometimes, predict the time slips even slips even though it was all but impossible to control his thoughts.

The appointment went much as Jason had anticipated. The doctor was understanding listened patiently to the story of his episodes. He explained that what Jason was experiencing was not that uncommon—in fact many patients suffered worse delusion when under extreme stress. He showed Jason various relaxation techniques and gave him so literature to read. Jason left feeling, as he had expected that the appointment had been both a waste of time and money.

Finally, a method of proving he matter to Katy came to mind. It was so simple that he couldn't believe he hadn't thought of it earlier. It was 2 AM but he was so excited to tell his wife that he had a difficult time in going back to sleep.

Chapter 4

Jason awakened early the next morning and waited anxiously for Katy to arise. He felt excited by the prospect 0f having someone who would believe him and share his burden, when she did get up words began pouring from his mouth at such a rate that she to halt him and force him to restart—and to proceed at a slower pace. Jason forced himself to calm down. His plan was simple. Katy was to write something on a piece of paper and not reveal her message to him. Jason would ask her to tell him what she had written. And she was to comply. Then Jason would concentrate on the letters "NISS" and attempt to invoke a time slip. Jason, however, would remember and thus prove that something strange had indeed happened when he told her what she had written. Katy thought the whole thing was ridiculous but, largely in order to please Jason, she complied and the experiment went just as planned and that Jason should continue to see the psychiatrist. She insisted that she didn't hearing Jason's instructions about writing on the paper. Only then did Jason realize the fact that only he could remember the incident It was if had never happened for everyone else. He tried the whole test again but not the fact that he had told her to read what she had written, This time Katy remember his instructions to write on the paper but not the fact that he had then to read she had written. Katy was now as puzzled as he was. Jason was greatly relieved to know that he was not entirely subject to time slips but could indeed also invoke the same of his own volition. At the same time he was glad that to have an "accomplice who knew what he was going through. Incidentally Katy had written on the—"KISS sucks!" Jason couldn't help but agree that this was also his sentiment.

Jason went on to assure Katy that no one could be faulted for doubting him. Indeed it was doubtful whether anyone could believe him as he could scarcely believe the whole thing himself. Katy was scared but Jason himself was growing rather accustomed to the time slips. Jason them. He then explained again what had happened and tried to form an analogy with which he got nowhere. Finally he compared the situation to an old phonograph record which one could play but which would sometimes skip wkip backwards and play the same track or groove over again. Again there were countless questions to ask but no answers. What had caused him to develop that strange ability in the first place? Would the ability go away in time? Would 60 seconds always be the duration of the time slips/ Why was he now able to bring on the episodes when desired. The questions went on and on with no answers.

Jason remembered a discussion in college about time. He didn't remember much of what had been said but he did recall that time is not the simple concept that people accepted. He would have to consult some books about the nature of time. Regardless of what he found he knew that he would have some valuable information to add.

Chapter 5

Jason's musings were interrupted as Jeff came back to the breakfast table after using the bathroom. Jason felt that there was now more to tell Jeff and began discussing the issue again. He told Jeff to sit. Jeff immediately assumed that he had done something wrong but Jason was quick to do away with that notion. "No Jeff," he said. "if anything I wrong around here it's with me but I don't know what it is.

He then went to retell the story and left nothing out. Jeff's response to the whole affair was predictable, "Cool!" said.

The light response made Jason laugh. Perhaps he was taking the matter to seriously.

Next Jeff had his father repeat the note trick and was truly amazed when Jason recited his message which was much the same as Katy's had been except for the words. Jeff had written "Fuck NISS!" which expresses Jason's feelings also. Jason wanted to repeat the trick but Jeff was satisfied. Jason was encouraged by how quickly he was able to invoke tine slips this time. It was only a matter of concentrating on the letters for a few seconds.

"Hey dad, I've got an idea. "spoke up Jeff.: if these things last for 60 seconds you could make some money in Las Vegas. Aren't we concerned with money right now?

"We don't need money that bad," interjected Katy.

"Oh, but we will in a month," replied Jason. "It doesn't look like I'm going to find a job anytime soon and we can't live on what you bring home. Maybe I could win at least enough to get us by for a while." Katy was dead set against the plan—particularly since it involved Jason going by himself

"Well, take some time off and come with me," said Jason.

"I can't d that right now—we're too busy," protested Katy.

"Well, if we wait a month we'll be in a real financial bind," reminded Jason.

"I'll go with you, dad, "chimed in Jeff.

"No you won't," interposed Kay. You've got final exams next week and scholarships to think of. Besides that you're not old enough to get in the casinos."

Finally, it was decided that Jason would have to indeed go alone. He would, however, call every night and check in. That decision having been made, Jason decided that a few preparations were in order. He didn't want the IRS to get any of his money so he would have to carry it with him or cash out each time before he reached the $600 level. First of all he went to a specialty store that carried money belts. He selected a belt that would accommodate a lot of bills—the advertisement stated that it would hold 10,000 dollars. Jason severely doubted this as, even with hundred dollar denominations, the belt would have to accommodate 1000 of the belts. It would be so thick by thn that that everyone would know he was wearing a money belt anyway and the show purpose would have been defeated. The problem was that the treasury had discontinued making bills larger that 100 dollars in 1969. If this were not the case a money belt could probably hold a million dollars. Finally, Jason decided to forego the belt altogether and simply purchased two small backpacks—actually daypacks which would not look out of place for a vacationer. He had considered taking his attaché case but had been too many movies with attaché cases that were full of money. Two day packs seemed to be overdoing it but Jason bought them anyway. A god sized fanny pack might have sufficed but Jason hated them -calling them "pseudo-colostomy" bags.

Next Jason went to a gun shop—Big Al's Pistol and Rifle Center. The store had a small shooting range for buyers who wanted to try out their weapons. Jason was well aware of the fact that he would never be able to carry a sidearm while gambling in a casino.

He would leave the pistol in a day pack and put the pack on the floor while he was playing, The purpose of the weapon was to protect him while he wasn't gambling. He intended to wear a light sports jacket and would then be able to simply stick the gun in a coat pocket or in his belt for that manner as it would not be visible. He would also sleep with the gun. He was, perhaps, being overcautious because he did realize that he would probably be able to undo a robbery if such should occur merely by forcing a time slip. Nevertheless, he wanted protection as he anticipated winning a lot of money. Jason already possessed 5 pistols but they were too large to serve his purpose. With Al's help he finally selected a Charter Arms .38 Special snub-nosed five shot revolver. Five rounds should be plenty to discourage anyone with robbery on their mind and accuracy would certainly not be a problem. Jason took the gun to the range and was able to hit a 1-foot target at 30 feet 9 out of 10 times. There was considerable kick but Jason was unfazed having shot a .45 a number of times in Vietnam. He had, in fact, killed two Viet Cong with the weapon. In addition, he owned a .44 Magnum which kicked like a mule.

It was decided that Jason would leave the following morning. There was no use in procrastinating the matter. He gathered as much money as he could—depleting their checking account and taking whatever cash advances he could on their credit cards. In addition, he withdrew the $10,000 they had in their savings account and which was intended for Jim's next tuition payment. He then left Katy enough money for groceries for a couple of weeks. This accomplished, Jason went to bed, intending to arise at 3 AM and depart. He hoped to be able to make the drive in one day even though the distance was about 900 miles. He calculated that 15 hours would be required.

Before Jason knew it the alarm was buzzing and it was time to get up. Jason shaved and showered and was ready to go at 3:30 AM. Katy had also gotten up and fixed some bacon and eggs. Jason found an old thermos bottle and filled it with fresh coffee. It was now time to leave and Jason kissed Katy good bye. She was in tears but Jason reassured her that everything would work out.

After an exhausting drive across Colorado, Wyoming and Utah he finally reached Las Vegas at 8:30 PM. He had made the drive in

16 hours with stops for a couple of meals and gas. It was Sunday, May 29, 2005 and the day before Jason's birthday His are would be 48—too young to retire unless he was either an army lifer or a police officer. Jason planned on spending several weeks in Vegas although he hadn't mentioned this to his family. For one thing he didn't want to acquire his money so rapidly as to attract attention, He actually didn't consider himself a gambler although he did know the basics of the most of the games. With is 60 second replay ability it was difficult to imagine how he could possibly lose. However, he certainly couldn't allow himself to win every hand.

Chapter 6

It was rather hot in Vegas but not really uncomfortable. One thing about Las Vegas—it was never humid or sticky—unlike the jungles of Vietnam some 25 years earlier. It was just hot and dry. Jason was already missing Katy. They had made love the night before and he was still marveling at the intensity involved.

Jason began to formulate a plan. First of all he would try the slots. He would begin by inserting coins in a machine. Most of the machines now accepted bills also—unlike the old days. When he hit a jackpot he would slip back 60 second and redo the spin after betting the maximum amount. He planned to keep track of the last symbol displayed on the rightmost reel in order to know when a jackpot spin was coming. He might miss on occasion but he could always slip back again if necessary. He could handle Blackjack in much the same fashion. He didn't know much about playing craps but would learn. His favorite card game was Texas Hold'em and he planned to spend a lot of time at those table. Roulette was one game that Jason was really counting on. He would watch one game and then slide back and redo his bet. He should be able to double his money simply by betting odd/even or red/black. He also planned to depend heavily on Keno. One problem with the latter game was that 60 seconds just wasn't enough. He would possibly have to go back several minutes once he found out what number he needed to select. He conducted a little experiment that involved piggybacking time slips to determine if this was feasible. With the help of his watch, he determined that this was indeed possible. This meant that the amount of time he could go back was actually unlimited in a sense. He would age only 1 minute while performing multiple time slips.

Jason checked into a hotel on Fremont Avenue in the downtown area and got a decent room He planned to live comfortably but not lavishly. He quickly took a shower and considered going out to gamble for a while but decided that he was just too tired and to postpone his debut until the next morning. Je final decided to visit the liquor store next to the hotel and purchase a bottle of vodka and some Collins mix. This done, he mixed himself a drink, getting ice from a dispenser at the end of the hotel floor. He then sipped his drink while thinking about what say ahead for him. He did have a swim suit so he donned it and went down to the lobby and the swimming pool. He didn't intend to do any swimming but wanted to soak in the hotel's jetted pool. He made himself comfortable in the hot water- too comfortable and he dozed off and suddenly found his head underwater. He began sputtering and coughing and looked around to see if anyone had been watching. Directly opposite him in the spa pool was a pretty girl who was laughing and obviously at him. He could do nothing but laugh himself and try to explain. Soon he was engaged in conversation with the young lady who proved to be a college student who was in Vegas with three friends for a week.

Jason slept until about 5 AM which was about normal for him. The earl morning hours were a good time to plan out the activities for the day as well as contemplate whatever needed to be contemplated. He considered the early morning as "his" time. At the present time Jason certainly had much to contemplate, He performed a series of pish-ups and sit-ups and then went outside to jog for a mile. The fact that he was going to be living a somewhat decadent life for a few weeks didn't mean that he should stop exercising. After his jog Jason showered and shaved. On this, his 48th birthday, he decided to start out the day with a good breakfast—steak and eggs in fact. As he didn't intend to return to his room before beginning to gamble, he put a roll of hundred-dollar bills in his pocket. He considered taking a daypack and the revolver with him but finally decided against it. He wanted to investigate, first of all to find out whether the casinos would allow him to retain a daypack while gambling. It seemed to him that this would be no different than allowing a woman to carry a purse. He suspected that the casinos would all have lockers were patrons could check their belongings but wanted to verify this. Perhaps he might have to purchase a padlock.

Many of the casinos served very cheap or even free breakfasts but Jason was in the modo for something more substantial. As he passed the concierge's desk he sked the man where he could get a good steak and egg breakfast. /the concierge replied that the restaurant right across the street was as good a place as any and Jason heeded his advice.

After a leisurely breakfast Jason walked the half block to the Golden Nugget casino where he planned to begin his day. He noted that some of the other gamblers carried backpacks so he walked back to this hotel and got one of is own along with the revolver which re thrust in the pack.

Seven AM found Jason back in the Golden Nugget where there were already many gamblers many having stayed out all night to pursue elusive fortunes. Jason found a simple three-reel slot machine where the top prize of $800 was paid to anyone who bet a dollar and then had the reels stop with red, white and blue 7s on a pay line. He inserted a 20-dollar bill and was thankful that the days of inserting nickels were gone. He went through the twenty without seeing potential win on any line and inserted second bill. This time he noticed the needed 7s on the bottom line—a line that he hadn't selected. He then concentrate on his magic letters—the name of his hated employer and stepped back in time where he waited for a cherry on the rightmost reel—a spin that had immediately preceded the three 7s. The machine made a hideous noise and Jason almost hit the floor—thinking he was back in Vietnam. Am employee arrived shortly and paid Jason his $800 in crisp new hundred-dollar bills. Having had enough of the slots Jason moved to an empty blackjack table. The dealer seemed overly friendly which was often the case or so it seemed. The minimum bet was $5 and Jason played about even for half an hour—then told the dealer that he had to go. Before leaving he hit a 21 and noted that his previous hand had been 2,2. Then he simply forced his way back in time and waited for the pair of deuces. Once he had played that hand he bet $500 on the next hand collected his $500 in winning chips and left the table after tipping the dealer. He proceeded to the cashier but cashed in only $550 worth of chips. He had read somewhere that the IRS insisted on being informed about cash-ins that amounted to $600 or more. He considered the matter further and decided to try to avoid the IRS. He wasn't being exactly patriotic but didn't want to go to the cashier every time ne neared the 600 dollar mark in winnings.

Next Jason decided to try some Texas Hold'dem. He suddenly realized that the trip to Vegas had been unnecessary as he could have simply played Hold'em on the Internet. He had done all right with his at home although he never reached the where he made a withdrawal. However, he reasoned that since he was in Vegas, he might as well use the time beneficially.

The game was actually quite simple. The object was to create the best poker hand possible from 7 cards—two hole cards and 5 "community" cards. Initially each player was dealt his two hole cards and a betting round ensued. Next three community cards were placed in the middle of the table. These cards were called the "flop" and the players bet again. The fourth card—the "turn" card was then dealt and a third betting round took place. Following that round the "river" card came out and the final betting round began.

Jason found that the poker table were in a separate large room at the Golden Nugget. He remembered about how Doyle Brunson, Amarillo Slim and some other guy had brought the game to Las Vegas in the 70s after inventing it in a small town in Texas. Within a short time it became very popular and was now called the "Cadillac of poker," Jason made a mental note to find out when and where the next World Series of Poker would take place.

On his way to the poker room Jason stopped at a roulette table. On a whim he bought some chips and put !00 dollars on the number 48—his newly achieved age. The wheel came up with a 26 so he forced a time slip and found that the wheel had not yet been spun. He placed. He placed another 100 dollar chip but this time on number 26. In order to appear somewhat normal je placed a hundred dollars on each of four other numbers. When the wheel was spun and 26 was hit Jason tried his best to act excited but was not very successful. "Oh well," he thought. "I've got to practice that."

It was then noon and Jason had been playing Hold'em for three hours. On occasion he lost purposely but won perhaps too often as players kept leaving the table. He tried to avoid time slips but resorted to them on occasion when he suspected a bluff. Even this didn't help when the bluffer failed to show his cards after a successful bluff. Jason found that he felt somewhat guilty about having used time slips during his Hold'em session and decided to avoid them in the future. He didn't feel at all guilty about taking money from the casinos but didn't want to take advantage of his fellow gamblers. He would avoid using time slips while playing Hold'em and attempt to win with the skills that he had. However, if he happened to end up in a one-on-one situation with a rude player or a bully he wouldn't hesitate invoke a slip and punish that player.

Jason found that he was now hungry and had a craving for some good Mexican food. He went back to his hotel and got in his car, intending to drive to the strip where we was told there were several good Mexican restaurant. He found one of the restaurants he had been told about and entered the establishment. While waiting for his food Jason consumed a couple of large margaritas and was feeling not pain. He realized that he was going to have to watch himself or he would return home as a raging alcoholic.

For lunch Jason had three enchiladas—one cheese, one beef and one chicken. After, more or less, inhaling is food he drove back to the hotel and took a two-hour nap, He felt good when he got up—the alcohol fortunately not affecting him. For the rest of the day Jason entertained himself by driving around the city and looking at the sights. It had been some ten years since he had been in Vegas and there had certainly been a lot of building going on. Among other destinations Jason drove out to the Hoover Dam on Lake Mead. The dam was just 30 miles southeast of the city so a short drive was required. At the time of its construction in the 30s it had been the largest dam in the world. Ninety-six men were killed during. Jaspits construction. Jason paid the seven-dollar fee and was able to actually go inside the dam which he found extremely interesting despite his preoccupation with gambling.

Jason spent the next two days on Fremont Street playing mostly Hold'em at the Golden Nugget, the Fremont, the Stratosphere, El Cortez and several other casinos. During his breads from the Hold'em tables he would play some blackjack or entertain himself at a roulette table. At the latter he bet mostly either red/black or odd/even. The fact that something was going on was just too evident when he placed a large sum on a single number. He began each day with an exercise session followed by a mile of jogging.

On Thursday Jason moved from his hotel to the Mirage on the strip. Before embarking to gamble he put $2,000 in his pocket to get him onto a Hold'em table. He found that the Mirage itself seemed to be a good poker site. Over a period of 3 hours he won some $7,000 dollars without using a time slip so he was quite satisfied and quit at 9 PM. He then cashed in his chips and visited the men's room where he deposited his cash his daypack. After having his pack locked in the hotel safe he swam for a half-hour and then soaked his aching muscles in a jacuzzi. He couldn't understand why his muscles were sore and the best he could come up with was that he had been unconsciously tightening various muscles—particularly those in his back and neck. Now Doyle Brunson would undoubtedly note that Jason was unable to keep from tightening his muscles at certain times. He had to avoid this "tell."

Jason decided to avoid the downtown casinos for the remainder of his trip. The real money was in the behemoth casinos on the strip. These were so large and affluent that one customer's winnings couldn't phase them.

Friday was largely a repeat of the previous day. Jason played Hold'em at Caesars and several other large casinos and everything went according to plan. At about 4 PM he suddenly realized that he was famished -not having anything to eat since breakfast at the Mirage. He found that he was in the mood for some good seafood. The concierge at the Mirage recommended a restaurant that a little over 2 miles away—somewhat father than Jason wanted to walk so he went to his room and got his car keys. He began driving through a

THE SIXTY SECONDS

rather seedy area of town, He was stopped at a light when a black male walked up to the passenger window with a revolver and demanded Jason's wallet. Jason concentrated on the magic letters and, he next thing he knew, the was just stepping off the curb. By the time he reached the open car window he was staring down the barrel of a ,38 social. He groped for words and then stumbled away in confusion. Jason had simply drawn the gun from a jacket pocket. He had noted that a sport coat with levis was common attire in Vega. Jason wasn't carrying that much money but still didn't intend to be robbed.

Finally, he entered the restaurant and took a seat neat the exit and facing the entrance. Perhaps he had watched too many western movies where the heroic gunfighter did the same thing but he did feel safer that way. A waitress brought him a menu and he was surprised at the large selection. Then the cook himself came out and asked if he could be of assistance. Jason was a little overwhelmed and asked the cook what he would recommend. The cook told Jason that, if he like swordfish he couldn't go wrong with that selection. Jason had indeed had swordfish steak on one occasion and liked it very much so he opted for that choice.

Although the restaurant was quite busy, Jason's food arrived in minutes and was hot that he couldn't immediately start eating. Once he did begin all else was forgotten. The steak was far superior to the on he had previously had. Whereas that one had been good it had also been a little chewy. This one melted in Jason' mouth. After finishing the last bite he left a generous and waved to the chef whom he could see in the half-open cooking area.

On the drive back to the Mirage Jason placed the revolver on the passenger seat so that it would be handy. He closed the windows, relying on the car's air conditioner which seem to quite adequate. He arrived at the hotel without incident and mixed up a Vodka Collins. Jason realized that it was now 8 PM at home and time to call Katy as he had been doing. She sounded worried and was relieved to hear that things were going well. Od course Jason did not tell her about the robbery attempt. She had no idea that he had a gun with him and would certainly have done all she could to prevent him from bringing it in the first place. Jeff was a different matter but Jason still didn't mention the incident. His concluding words were, "Cool Dad—see if you can bankrupt the strip. Those places have too much money anyway." Jason couldn't help but agree.

Jason was tired but his mind was racing and sleep elude him. He finally put a finger on what was bothering him. What lay in the future? Could anyone live as he had been living? If he were to die what would become of his family? In the middle of these questions he reached a conclusion. Originally, he had come to Las Vegas to win money to get by on until Jason found a job. Now he was aware of the fact that he might never get a job. There was also no telling where the time slips were leading him. He didn't know how long the strange ability would last nor what the time slips were doing to him. Everything pointed to one conclusion—he had to take advantage of the here and now in order to take care of his family for life. That meant retiring all debt as accumulating a considerable sum for the future. Frankly Jason never wanted to have to worry about money again. He would add up the money he had made thus far and pay taxes on it. It wasn't worth it.

Giving up on sleep, Jason went to the hotel's guest computer and began reading about the strip. Based on information from one site he compiled a list of all the major casinos on the strip and decided to hit three of them each remaining day. After he had alphabetized it his list read:

- Aladdin
- Barbary Coast
- Boardwalk
- Bourbon Street
- Caesar's Palace
- Circus Circud
- Ellis Island
- Excalibur
- Flamingo
- Frontier
- Hard Rock Café
- Harrah's

- Hotel San Reno
- Imperial Palace
- Klondike Inn
- Luxor
- Mandalay Bay
- MGM Grand
- Mirage
- Monte Carlo
- New York New York
- Psalms
- Paris
- Riol
- Riviera.
- Royal
- Sahara
- Stardust
- Stratosphere Tour
- Terribles
- Treasure Island
- Tropicna
- Tuscany
- Venetian
- Westin Casino
- Westward Ho
- Wynn

The list was somewhat outdate and some of the casinos were out of business. Also some of the newer ones weren't listed. It was now 11 PM but Jason still felt incapable of sleeping. He finally decide to undertake one more session of gambling but first decided to mix himself a vodka Collins. As his ice was melted he took the metal bucket and exited his room. He rounded a corner and was headed for the ice machine wen he heard a scream from down the hallway. "He's got my purse!" an attractive lady in an evening gown cried. Jason ran to her said and asked where the assailant had gone as not one was visible. "the elevator!' she cried and Jason looked to her side where the elevator was located. Nothing that it was going down, he opened the door to the stairwell and started down—taking two steps at a time. He wasn't sure where the robber would exit but assumed that he would go to the ground floor. He burst out of the stairwell at that level just as the elevator doors opened but it was empty. Jason then realized that only a time slip would enable him to catch the thief. Quickly he concentrate on the initials of his hated former employer and found that he was back in his room. The previous time he had taken a minute to put on a shirt but realized now that he didn't have time. Quickly he grabbed the metal bucket and emptied the water on the floor. He then emerged shirtless into the hallway. He turned the corner just in time to see the man grab the purse from the lady and spring into an open elevator. Jason reached the elevator just as the doors were closing and burst through, slamming the ice bucket into the man's face. The man fell backwards against the wall and Jason quickly planted a shoe into his genitals. As the man bent over in pain Jason repeated the blow with the bucket and connected with his forehead. The man collapsed on the elevator floor just as the doors were closing. Quickly Jason pushed the "Open" button and the door reopened to reveal the anxious victim of the robber. Jason handed her the purse with a smile and said, "I think this belongs to you. As she was thanking him a hotel security guard arrived on the scene and told them that would take care of things and notify the police.

After this singular interlude Jason found himself a bit shaken as he retrieved his now misshapen ice bucket. For the second time he headed for the ice machine and then returned to his room where he mixed the drink for which he was now more than ready.

Jason then decided to try one of the casinos on his list. He planned to get into some high stakes Hold-em games and he needed some experience with the latter. Before coming to Vegas he had never before played for stakes other that nickels, dimes or quarters online. Finally, he decoded to visit Caesar's Palace one more time. He was happy to see that a large number of high-stake games were going on. He decided to play at what game he could make the most money in the shortest amount so he started out with five-card stud. He played for several hours without even invoking a time slip. Jason had always been a decent poker player but now the big difference was that he didn't have to worry about losing—he had plenty of money... Basically he was the best player at the table so he didn't need time slips. When he finally left the table he was up by $3,000. At 1:30 AM Jason walked back to the Mirage and went t bed. This time he went quickly to sleep.

Chapter 7

The next morning Jason packed his suitcase and threw it into the trunk of his BMW. He retrieved his backpacks from the hotel safe and then checked out. He had discovered that the Aladdin had rooms for half the price he was paying at the Mirage. Although he could well afford to stay wherever he wanted he didn't want to become totally frivolous. He might as well save money whenever possible. The Aladdin was also the first casino on his list so he might as well tackle the casinos in order. He would skip Caesar's as he had already taken close to $20,000 from them. Before he went to his room he checked out the casino at the Aladdin. It was enormous. The Internet had mentioned something to the effect that the Allakikn had 100,000 square feet of casino space.

Jason was impressed by his room and even more impressed by the fact that there were 2500 such rooms. The place was like a small city. It contained seven restaurants so there would really be no need to go out for food. Jason felt the need for immediate action so he unpacked his suitcase. First he headed for the roulette tables. After losing several hundred dollars he placed 100 dollars on his number -48. The wheel was spun and the little ball ended up in the 11 slot. Jason then placed 500 dollars on number 11a and five hundred dollars on each of 5 other random numbers This time when the five was hit he yelled, "Yes!," as loud as he could. As the dealer started to give him large denomination chips, Jason said, "No—I'll take these." He then removed his baseball hat—a Yankee hat as had always idolized Babe Ruth, Lou Gehrig and especially Yogi Berra who had a nonpareil way with words. He pushed his chips into his hay and headed for the cashier. He cashed in for $20,000 and filled out his form for the IRS. the only player.

Next Jason went to a blackjack table where he was the He played only player. He played conservatively for a while, not even bothering with time slips. Finally, it was time to get busy so he upped his bets to a hundred dollars. He lost one hand and then won three in a row as he used time slips. He played for another half hour and then became bored and told the dealer that he was "all-in" and put all of his chips on the betting circle (some $20,000. The dealer laughed and said, "We're not playing Texas Hold'em."

"Just deal the cards," Jason said. Jason had to invoke five time slips to get back to a hand where he had been dealt a pair of aces. He hit both aces and got face cards with each one giving him two 21s. The dealer had a king and an eight so he was through and had to pay Jason $60,000. People were crowding around the table, anxious to see what Jason would do next but he colored up and left the table. He had to use his hat again as the largest denomination chips the dealer had were one thousands. As Jason left the dealer said, "There's a thousand dollar table in the high roller room. Jason followed his directions and reached a roped-off area where a guard asked him is he was really going to play—that observers weren't welcome. "I'm a player," replied Jason and meant in more ways than one as he intended to play with time.

"Well then—welcome to my abode," said the guard with a malicious grin. Jason immediately felt underdressed as many of the players wore suits. However, when he looked closer he saw that there were also players in shorts. He was sort of in the middle with his sports jacket, golf shirt and levis. Most of the games that were going on were Baccarat—a game that Jason had never played. He knew just the fundamentals. The idea was to get nine in two cards. This was a natural win. Eight was also a natural win and could only be beaten by a nine. If you went over nine you take another card. If you ended up with a 17 or whatever the one would be dropped. Face cards counted as ten and aces as one. Jason didn't understand the betting so he watched a hand. Apparently only two participants received cards—these were known as the banker and the player and the remaining participants bet on the cards of these two. Jason took a seat and tossed $500 on the table. He had seen this done before and the dealer quickly swooped in and converted the money to chips.

After a half-hour Jason was up by $10,000 even though he still didn't understand many things about the game. Some of the others were laughing at him but this didn't bother him and he laughed right along with them. He saw that exact amount wagered by a gentleman in a suit. However, the guy last the bet and Jason decided to push neither his luck nor his incipient time travelling abilities and tipped the dealer $500. From there he went to the cashier to cash in his chips and fill out his accustomed IRS form.

As he headed for the casino exit to the hotel he passed the Keno area. He hadn't yet tried the game and decided it was about time he did so. He realized that just going back 60 seconds wouldn't buy him anything. The numbers came out too slowly. He found out that he would have to piggyback time slips so that he could go back several minutes. When a new game was to start he would fill out a form but not get on it. Then he would perform the time slios until the correct game number was shown. Then he would get a new form and copy the old one. He immediately won the $15,000 for the game. He then continued for the exit but stopped a roulette table. He repeated his efforts of the previous day and walked away with 4800 dollars. The wheel operator looked at him as if he had been cheating but Jason merely said, "Can you believe that luck?

Chapter 8

By then Jason was ready for lunch and decided to try one of the Aladdin's seven restaurants. First however, he wanted to get one of his daypacks from the hotel safe and empty his pockets. He did so and, while he was it, asked the concierge for his recommendation as to where he should have lunch. He heeded the forthcoming advice and had a light but delicious lunch which featured smoked chicken strips which were very tender and tasty They were served with fries and a tangy sauce for the chicken. Following lunch Jason played the slot machines. He found the most expensive machine he could until hitting a jackpot. Then he would invoke a time slip as possible. After winning a large jackpot he suddenly heard a voice behind him. "How do you know when you're going to hit a big jackpot? It seems like that's the only time you bet big money." Jason turned and saw a pleasant looking man with sandy colored hair.

"I guess I just have a feel for," said Jason.

"You ought to try the big money machines," said the sandy haired one. They're roped off in the card just like the high roller card section. They do all they can you feel special. You notice how they offer you drinks out here. In the big money machine section you'll get a drink before you finish your old one,"

Jason shook hand with the man as they introduced each other. The man's name, or rather nickname was, appropriately enough, Sandy. "Let's see if my magic works for you," said Jason. He then had Sandy spin the wheels until he hit a decent jackpot on a line that was selected. Jason invoked a time slip and said, "It's going to hit next spin. Put in 10 dollars this time. Sandy did so and the machine hit a 500-dollar jackpot. Sandy insisted on sharing the jackpot with Jason but the latter would have none of that. "Let's hook up later for a drink," suggested Jason and Sandy agreed. Jason then headed for the big money slots section. An hour later he was $50,000 dollars richer and no one had bothered him except the waitresses who wanted to bring him drinks. As he was leaving Sandy walked up and they walked to the nearest bar together. Sandy was a lawyer from Arizona. He was divorced and going to be in town for a week. Jason told Sandy about his plan to make the rounds of the various casinos in Las Vegas and invited him to come along whenever he could. "Today is Tuesday. I'm going to spend the rest of the day here at the Aladdin. Tomorrow I'm going to hit the MGM Grand, the Tropicana and New York New York. Thursday it'll be the Excalibur, the Luxor and Mandalay Bay. Friday the Monte Carlo, Boardwalk and the Bellagio will host us. After that I've got at least 15 places in mind but I'll play them before I leave. I've got at least two weeks if I need them."

"From what I've seen you'll be a millionaire before the week is out," commented Sandy.

Jason was tired—tired from the exertion of forcing time slips and returned to his room for a nap. Although he was on the 10th floor it was easy to get to the lobby or the casino. The hotel was arranged so that no room was farther than 7 rooms away from an elevator. Jason slept for about two hours and awoke bright-eyed and refreshed. He planned on getting in a high stakes poker game that evening but first wanted a good steak. He phoned Sandy's room to see if he was hungry, Sandy replied that he was indeed hungry and that he was ready to go so the two of them planned to meet in the lobby in five minutes. Once there, they asked the concierge for advice and he recommended a place that was within the Aladdin complex. They took the short walk and were rewarded by a couple of excellent steaks. As they ate they talked and Jason learned that Sandy also had children in college—both at the University of Arizona—a girl was majoring in nursing and a son in law school. Sandy himself had been divorced for just over six months and had custody of the kids. He le liked to gamble but said he was too cheap to lose very much.

Upon returning to the Mirage Jason was ready for some high stakes poker. He became almost immediately involved in one of these. The minimum bet was 100 dollars and some of the bets were enormous. Jason amused himself by trying to play without time slips. Now that he could afford to do this he found it very entertaining. He didn't mind cheating the casinos but didn't like doing this to his fellow poker players with an occasional exception. He found that he enjoyed the camaraderie of most of the other players.

When the night was done Jason was up by just over $30K and had enjoyed himself thoroughly. There were also other winners but they did not seem to begrudge Jason his victories and no one had outdone him—he was proud of that fact. He vowed to do the rest of his poker playing in this fashion. He would use his time slips when he was pitted only against the house.

Chapter 9

The rest of the week consisted of some grueling days for Jason. He was often accompanied by Sandy the latter shied away from the high stake games that Jason actively sought out. Jason did take time to gamble with Sandy but didn't force him to take advantage of a time slip. Sandy was already suspicious and might well have intuited that was going on. One new game that

Jason attempted was craps. He didn't evet take time to learn the rules of the game. One problem was that it seemed that the bets were too small to interest him. He didn't like to bet too much more than the other gamblers. For this reason he was doing most of his gambling in the high roller rooms. Most of the casinos had high stakes no-limit Texas Hold'em tables in a special area. Limit or pot-limit Hold-em didn't interest Jason at all. A large bet on a no-limit table was not at all out of place—in fact it was the norm

Jason finally made a decision but was afraid it would leave Sandy out of the picture but was afraid it would leave Sandy out of the picture to a large extent. He wanted to get his money amassed and be done with it. Then he would be able to relax without having to worry about time slips. To this end he began rushing from one casino to another—seeking the high roller rooms or the elite slot machines. On Wednesday Jason and Sandy visited the MGM Grande, the Tropicana and New York New York. On Thursday they had breakfast together and Jason old Sandy of what he had in mind. To his surprise, Sandy still wanted to accompany him.

"I wanted to see Vegas and that's what I'll be doing," he said. "I can always find something to entertain me while you do your high rolling."

"Well, let's get moving," said Jason. I've got a car and I think we'll take it today," The entire day was spent on the move and the duo hit the Excalibur, the Luxor, the Mandalay, the Monte Carlo, Boardwalk and the Bellagio. Jason left a daypack in the car and they twice had to make trips to Jason's BMW to empty the day pack into the larger backpack that he kept locked in the trunk. They were very surreptitious about this to ensure that no one saw what they were doing. Car trunks were just not all that safe from a determined burglar. By the time they finished for the day all of Jason's pockets were crammed full of hundred-dollar bills as they hadn't taken a backback to the Bellagio. Back at the Aladdin Jason took care of the money and he and Jason went out to get something to eat. Jason insisted on buying though Sandy protested. You don't know how much money I made today—as a matter of fact I don't either.

"I know how many trips you made to your car to unload," responded sandy. After a late dinner Jason headed for the Luxor with sand tagging along, This time he tried playing with the benefit of any time slips whatsoever but it didn't see, to matter as he soon found himself up by $12,000. Perhaps he could play poker for a living if nothing else worked out. He already had plans to sign up for a World Series of Poker event in a few months.

The next day, which was Friday, Jason and Sandy hit the Psalms, the Gold Coast, the Rio, Casear's palace again and Treasure Island. Jason was immensely successful and began to think of going home. He was tired of the concentration needed to force one time slip after another.

After they had completed the circuit Jason invited Sandy to his room. Before doing so had retrieved his other backpack from the trunk of his car. Now he dumped all the money on the bed, dove in and began wallowing in hundred-dollar bills. Sandy went to his room and got his camcorder—then filmed Jason's antics while promising to copy the footage to a DVD and send a copy to Jason. Jason didn't have a DVD player but he would certainly get one now.

Feeling a little foolish, Jason got up and set about organizing the bills. He started making stacks on the table but was soon forced to the floor. Most of the bills were hundreds but there were bills of smaller denominations and they stacked them in separate stacks. JasOn opened a box of oversized rubber bands and they began making packages on the bills. As he packaged he counted and found his grand total to be 925,685 dollars—not bad at all. Once he was finished he put the money back in the backpack and called Katy. He told her that he was "halfway there." She wanted to know what "halfway" meant but he was elusive—telling her only that he would be done in a few days and coming home.

Jason suspected that Sandy might be tiring of the frenetic pace he was setting and stated so at breakfast on Saturday morning. "Just hurry up and eat," said Sandy. "We.ve got a lot of ground to cover today. By the way I am up $50,000 for the trip thanks to you and I' not complaining. I know I could have a lot more if I'd let you help me more but I'm certainly not complaining."

"Well, let's see if we can't send you back to Phoenix with a hundred thousand," stated Jason.

Sandy just shook his head. "I'm just amazed that you haven't been blacklisted yet. In fact, you're lucky that you're not at the bottom of Lake Mead in a pair of cement shoes."

"I'm well aware of that," admitted Jason. I have been, shall we say, "invited" to leave about six casinos. That's why I don't stay at any single one very long. I don't have a death wish and my mother didn't raise any fools.

"I still don't know how you do it," remarked Sandy. "Don't you think it's about time you told me.

"Yes it is," admitted Jason—"but you'll think I'm crazy. I know that I can trust you though, so I'll show you're the proof the same way I showed my wife and son. Jason felt a need to share his burden and he felt instinctively that he could trust Sandy. He got a piece pf paper and a pen and then went through the same procedure he had with Katy and Jeff.

Once he had Sandy thoroughly baffled he admitted that he was able to go back in time

"So now you know how I'm winning—I'm basically a cheat," he continued. He then went on to explain to Sandy how he had discovered that he could get by without the time slips while playing Hold'em.

"You don't have to do that." commented Sandy, "but it's admirable that you do. Afterall you're just using your God-given abilities."

"I have no idea how God enters the picture," admitted Jason.

"I'm sure you'll find out when the time is right," said Sandy. The two of them went on to discuss religion for a while and found that they had a lot in common although neither of them was a member of an organized church.

After breakfast the two of them left the Aladdin and drove to a bank and cashed in most of their money for cashier's checks. They two wired these to their respective banks. Jason retained $200,000 to play with and Sandy, 50,000. Jason put on the larger backpack while Sandy slung the daypack over a shoulder. While the had the Jason planned to visit the casinos at the far end of the strip. They parked at Circus Circus and spent about two hours there. Then they moved on to the Stratosphere Tower, the Sahara, the Riviera and the Hilton. At the Hilton they ate a well-deserved late lunch. After eating they had a drink and relaxed for a while. Sandy admitted that he could use some more cash and Jason suggested that they get in a blackjack game after they decided on a signal. In order to keep it simple Jason suggested that he would take his hands off the table whenever the dealer broke. That would Sandy could hit until he was in position to break and then stay. In order to avoid the suspicion of collusion Jason would also break of course before the dealer and lose the hand but his bets would be smaller than Sandy's. After an hour Sandy left–up by about $40,000 and Jason got up shortly afterwards telling the dealer that he didn't like to play alone. The two of them met up outside and Jason asked Sandy if he wanted more.

"Maybe tomorrow," replied Sandy. Jason and Sandy spent the rest of Saturday at Westward Ho and the Stardust. Jason had to empty his pockets to cover some large bets from some affluent Hold'em players but he still didn't use a time slip and won. He felt a lot more secure now that he knew had over $700,000 waiting for him at home and he lost several big hands intentionally.

The two of them had just arrived at Jason's car when two men got out of car about 30 feet away. They approached Jason and Simon rapidly and there was some threatening about them. Jason began to fumble for his .38 bit it was buried beneath money in his backpack which was hanging by a strap from his shoulder. "Okay Gentlemen, one of the men said a large Afro American with huge biceps which he displayed with a muscle shirt. "Time to pay the piper." Before Jason had time to react Sandy was in motion. A spinning back kick from Sandy laid the man out on the asphalt. The second man lunged at Sandy but the latter simply moved an chopped at the man's neck sending him sprawling. "Le me have him," interjected Jason. "Can't let you have all the fun," The second man got up shakily and threw a punch at Jason that he easily avoided. He threw two sharp left jabs and followed these with a straight right that rendered the man unconscious.

Very nice," praised Sandy. "Where did you learn that?"

"I was light-heavy-weight boxing champion of Scofield barracks in Hawaii after I got out of Vietnam," replied Jason. "And where did you learn that kick by the way."

"Well, I'm the reigning karate champion of Phoenix for my age," return Sandy. Once they arrived at the Aladdin that night Jason got and Sandy got their backs from the trunk of the BRW. Their takes for the day were $425,000 and $120,000 respectively. Almost everything was in hundred-dollar bills. After visiting the office had having their packs locked up Jason called Katy. He told her that he had wired some money and that she could check the balance the next morning. He refused to tell her how much was in the account but did say that she would be pleasantly surprised. She wanted to know when he would be back. He said simply that it would not be that much longer. He reassured her that he was fine—just tired and ready to come home.

"Just come home," she begged. We'll be all right. The idea was very tempting. Even after taxes Jason would have well over a million dollars and would be able to eliminate their indebtedness including the home mortgage. With the remainder of the money and Katy's income they could live comfortably until Jason found something. The one factor that augured against going home was the boy's education. Jim still had one year remaining until he got his bachelor's degree and two more years if he were to go on to law school. Jeff would be entering college in a year. He had good grades but they couldn't count on a scholarship. Still thinking of his family and missing them Jason went to sleep

Chapter 10

Jason awakened early, got his workout, and was ready to go by the time Sandy showed up for breakfast. "You may want to back off today, Sandy," said Jason in lieu of 'Good morning.' "I intend to go like hell today. My goal is to leave tomorrow—in fact right after I get you on a plane," Sandy had already informed Jason that he as flying out the next day.

"Well, first of all you don't have to worry about getting me on a plane," said Sandy. "That's what taxis are for. Secondly I don't have anything else to do today so I might as well chase you as anything else."

"I'm going to push today so I may get us kicked out of some places," warned Jason.

"No, you'll get kicked out but I'll just leave on my own," corrected Sandy. "I'm not going into any of those high roller rooms with you. Their plan for the day was simple. They would simply hit as many casinos as possible. They would start with six casinos that were almost in a row. These were Wyan's resort, the Venetian, the Imperial Palace, the Flamingo, Barbary Coast and Bourbon Street. Actually, if they spent time at all of these they would have put in a good day's work.

From the very start Jason was true to his word. He went for the jugular and jade it clear that he was out to gamble. He still forced himself too lose some pots but not as many as he normally did. He was actually asked to leave two establishments but by that time the damage had been done and he was far ahead of the game. He

THE SIXTY SECONDS

had gone to the men's room four times to empty his pockets into his backpack and the latter was bulging. They walked back to the Aladdin for lunch and a quick nap. Jason found, however, that he was too pumped up to sleep and went down to the Aladdin's casino. There he played aggressively and won some $90,000 at Keno. He was then "asked" to vacate the premises. He cashed in his chips and returned to his room. After emptying his pockets he would he had already made $300,000 that day. This was a record and he still had lots of time to play.

Jason had planned to let Sandy sleep but a knock on his hotel door came while Jason was returning the money to the backpack. Not sure if this was Sandy or not, Jason opened the door with his .38 In hand. Sandy stepped back and laughingly said, "Take it easy, dirty Harry!"

Since this would be their last chance Jason urged Sandy to let him help out with some time manipulation but Sandy refused, saying "I don't really need more money—after all I am a lucrative lawyer. You take care of yourself."

That afternoon they began with the Imperial Palace where Jason was a killer. He expected to be asked to leave but it didn't happen. Once again his strategic losses recued him or so he came to believe. Sandy was all excited because he had experienced a run of luck at a blackjack table. "You should have seen me, Jason," he exclaimed. "I was just like you."

Next they moved on to the Flamingo, the Barbary Coast and finally Bourbon Street. When they had finished their work at these casinos Jason was ready to call it quits. It was 4:30 in the afternoon and Jason calculated that if they hurried, they could make it to the Western Union station before it closed. They had both packs in the trunk and Jason wanted the money to be on its way to Longmont. Sandy also wanted to wire his money to Phoenix. The traffic was a problem but they finally make it to the station. The clerk there looked on in awe as Jason and Sandy emptied their packs. Jason had all his money in the larger backpack while Sandy was using the daypack. They began counting out the money and Jason had a total of almost 2 million dollars while Sandy had about $250,000. Jason sent all of his money except for $5,000 with which he planned to play one last session of Hold'em. In addition, he still needed to pay for his room and required some money for the trip home.

As they drove back to the Aladdin Jason felt a great sense of relief. The pressure was off—not only the pressure to win but the pressure to make financial ends meet. He still needed—or at least wanted a job but this was no longer a pressing need. If what Sandy said was true and there were indeed jobs in Arizona he might well move there. Katy could actually retire as could Jason for that matter. He and Katy had always loved Arizona anyway—particularly after visiting the Grand Canyon shortly before Jim was born. It was only NISS that kept them in Colorado. Many people hated the heat of Arizona but Jason thrived on it. A swimming pool would be almost a necessity but both Jason and Katy had always loved to swim. A great deal depended upon where Jeff would go to college. Jason wasn't sure whether if his mind were really bet on the University of Denver of if he were just intentionally trying to keep down college expenses. Jim had two semesters left was wasn't sire whether or not he wanted to enroll in the school of law.

That night Jason and Sandy ate at the Hard Rock Café and the food was surprisingly good. After they finished Sandy wanted to visit the Hard Rock casino and Jason didn't mind. He decided to make this his last session—win or lose. He sat at a blackjack table for several hours but ended up losing a hundred dollars as he didn't make use of his time travelling abilities. As he left the table Sandy walked up laughing. "That dealer doesn't have a clue as to how lucky he is," he said. Exhausted by their marathon day, Jason and Sandy drove back to the Aladdin and were soon in bed. Sandy had to be at the airport by 9 AM and Jason insisted, of course upon driving him.

Chapter 11

Jason arose at 6 AM, did his workout and then shaved and showered. He wanted to make sure to get Sandy to the airport in plenty of time. Sandy was ready and they found themselves in a position to have a somewhat leisurely breakfast. Little was said as they ate. Both felt that a blossoming friendship was coming to an end. Once they reached the airport they were talking and Jason walked with his friend into the terminal building. After Sandy had checked his sole suitcase Jason continued the conversation. "You know, Katy and I have always loved Arizona."

"People always seem to like it if they can deal with the heat," said Sandy.

"I guess what I'm saying," continued Jason. "if that it's not beyond the realm of possibility that we might move down there—especially if I can find a job. Katy can pretty much find a job wherever there's a hospital.

"Well, I sure would be happy to have you as neighbors," said Sandy, "and I'll look around and see what's available as far as jobs. I know quite a few people in your industry including some former clients. Fax me a copy of your resume when you get a chance." The two exchange phone numbers and email addresses and promised to keep in touch. When the time came to board the plane, Jason found himself almost om tears as he embraced Sandy. "You have a safe flight." Was all he could say.

"And you have a save drive," countered Sandy.

As Jason pulled away he felt truly alone. He inserted a CD in the player and began the long drive. This time he would take two days as there was really no hurry. Back in the old days he would have tried to make it in one day in order to avoid the cost of a motel room but he now didn't have to worry about that. The oil was fine, the radiator full and the tires properly inflated. The BMW might be ten years old but Jason had taken good care of it and, in return, had a good, dependable means of transportation.

All went well until he reached the barren stretch in Utah between Beaver and Nephi. There he caught himself dozing off and finally stopped at a rest area. There he did several wind sprints—a tactic he used with success in the past. This time, however the measure didn't seem to work and Jason decided to take a nap at the next rest area. Just as neared am overpass he suddenly found himself veering off the freeway and into an open field. His first thought was that he was going to roll—then he was back on the freeway and wide awake. He was sufficiently frightened by what might have been that he no longer needed to stop for a nap. A time slip had happened again and Jason was saved. This was now twice when that the slips had rescued him. He couldn't count on them again—rather he had to watch out for himself. He suddenly had a new thought. Perhaps everyone was going through time slips but couldn't remember them. For instance, another driver might have dozed off and left the road. However, he would be totally unaware of this and would therefore be doomed to repeat the mistake.

As Jason continued to drive he contemplated the time slips further. It was obvious that he was seeing just a tiny percentage of them. What was their cumulative effect on people? Must not earth's time be slowing down to accommodate the time slips? In other words must not a man be older that his established age due to the myriad of sixty second redos? He had not noticed a clock during a slip nor had he looked at his watch and wondered if the minute hand had jumped backwards? Did this make any difference anyway?

The countless questions were driving Jason insane and he did his best to think about something else. He pictured Katy's face when she called the bank that day to check on their balance. Of course she might get the same information from the Internet and would most likely do so. He pictured getting letters from creditors showing zero balances. He went pm to imagine himself going through their liabilities folder and paying off everything in full. He then pictured Jeff's animated face as Jason told him about playing with the high rollers. With such thoughts he finally rolled into Salt Lake City and concluded his first day on the road. He got a room at a Comfort Inn–a motel chain that he liked. He then went next door to a restaurant and had a dinner of liver and onions which really "hit the spot."

At 6:00 the next morning Jason once again on the road. He first stopped at a 24-hour gas station and filled up the BMW and purchased a new thermos which he filled with coffee. He wasn't hungry so he didn't bother with breakfast even though the motel offered a free meal. He did, however, grab an apple and a banana for the road. This time he was on the home stretch and the miles few by quickly. At 4 PM he took the exit for Longmont and, in a matter of minutes was pulling into his driveway. Katy came running out to greet him and they embraced passionately.

"I was so worried about you," she said. "you could have been robbed or who knows what?"

"I was fine the whole time," explained Jason. "I made a friend and we spent almost the whole time together." Katy wanted to know all about Sandy and Jason was more that willing to talk about him

"Your two will have to stay in touch," she said. "Good friends are hard to come by,"

"I hope to do more than just talk on the phone with," Jason said somewhat mysteriously, "but we'll talk about that more later. "Have you got any coffee—that's what I need, he continued, "Then I've got some bills to pay."

Chapter 12

"Hey Katy—did you ever call the bank?" asked Jason the next morning as she fixed breakfast. She was taking a day of vacation as she wanted to spend the day with Jason.

"No," she replied. "All I've been doing is worrying about you."

"Well call them—you might be surprised at what I've made."

"Well, I hope it's enough to make a dent in that stack of bills on the table," said Katy. "That'll take quite a was of cash right there. Anyway, the bank's not open yet but I can go online and check on our account. I got us set up for online banking last week. I've been going to do that for a long time bit I haven't tried it yet."

Katy went upstairs to get on the computer and Jason sat back to wait. A few minutes later Katy came downstairs with a look of disgust on her face. "Our account is all screwed up," she complained. "They're trying to tell me we have almost 2 million dollars in it. I wish we did—we'd pay off everybody and have all kinds of money left over."

"Well, let's start paying those vultures off," said Jason "because that figure is right.

Katy let out a shriek and threw her arms around Jason's neck, "How did you do it," she said over and over again.

"I think I pushed my lucky a little," replied Jason. "We'll take Jeff out and go celebrate tonight." Jason ate some pancakes and bacon and then cleared the table and sorted through the stack of bills. Then he went up to the study and retrieved the contents of a folder labeled "Current Liabilities." While he was at it he also emptied the "Long—Term Liabilities" folder. What he ended up with was quite an imposing stack of bills. The next thing they did was to fetch all seven of their credit cards. As they were all at their limit, neither of them carried the cards. Jason found a bill for each card among the stack on the table. He took them one by one and made a payment—not the minimum that was due or overdue but the entire outstanding balance. Katy enjoyed this very much and sat by with a pair of scissors to cut up each card as Jason finished with it. After Jason was finished with the credit cards he locate the home equity loan statement. It had a total of about $75,000 outstanding and Jason quickly wrote out a check to cover that amount. He considered paying off the house but decided to wait until they had a chance to talk about possibly moving to Arizona.

For the next order of business Jason needed the telephone. He called to get the payoff amount for the boy's automobiles. The BMW was paid off. Katy's Suburu Outback came next and Jason wrote a check of just over $15,000 for that vehicle. By then the stack of bills had shrunk to nothing instead there was a stack of receipts with each item marled "Paid."

"Well, now that you've paid everything in sight do you think we can afford a few groceries," asked Katy.

"I think we can manage that," replied Jason "and I think I could use a home-cooked meal for a change. We'll go out tomorrow night."

"Another thing we've got to do tonight is call Jim," said Katy. We've got so much to tell him. I didn't tell you but I guess there's a chance that he might be getting his scholarship back. The professor who disqualified him is in all kinds of trouble.

Jason and Katy spent a quiet but enjoyable afternoon together. They did go grocery shopping and, well before Jeff got home from school, they made love. Jeff finally came rolling in abut 4:00 PM. He immediately ran in and gave his dad a hug. After that the questions were nonstop. Jeff wanted to know exactly how much Jason had won but Jason was elusive in his answer, He did say, however, that he would not be okay without a job for a while. While he was thinking about it he called his headhunter and asked him if he found any new leads. The headhunter said that there seemed to be nothing in Denver and that perhaps he should think about relocating. Jason then asked him if he had heard anything about Arizona. John, the headhunter, replied that the Phoenix area was supposedly booming. This excited Jason as Sandy lived just outside Phoenix in Scottsdale.

A little later they called Jim. He was extremely excited to hear from them aa he had been considerably worried about is father. He knew only that Jason had lost his job and had taken off to Las Vegas in an attempt to win enough money to last until he could find another job. This had upset Jim as he had assumed that his father intended to cheat. Katy had assured him that this wasn't the case but he wanted to know all the details. When Jason told him about the time slips and how he had learned to invoke them, Jim was somewhat skeptical and Jason could hardly blame him. He simply told him to ask his mother and that this would provide proof. He offered to prove it over the phone but Jim said that this would not be necessary. He told Jason that he was indeed going to get his scholarship reinstated for his remaining two semesters so he would no longer be a financial burden. Of course, room and board still had to be paid for and these weren't cheap. Getting the scholarship back was a matter pf pride more than anything else.

That evening Jason broached the subject of relocation to Katy. "There are no jobs here," he said. "I talked to my headhunter this morning and he told me that the Denver area is one of the worst in the country as far as jobs in software engineering, what do you think about moving?"

"Well, I suppose there's nothing holding us here," said Katy. "Our parents have passed on and our brothers and sisters ae spread all over the country. Do you have any idea where we might go?"

"As a matter of fact I do," answered Jason. I told you about the friend I made in Vegas—Sandy. Well he happens live in Scottsdale, Arizona which is just a suburb of Phoenix. He told me that the Phoenix area is a hot spot for computer programmers and my headhunter told me the same thing. I think we ought to sell our house and move there,"

Katy seemed to approve of the idea so they decided to sleep on it and then talk to Jeff to see how he felt about it. Jeff had just broken up with his "true love" so they didn't expect that he would have many objections. If they were all in agreement they would call Jim.

Chapter 13

Jason got up at 5 AM

www.ingramcontent.com/pod-product-compliance
Lightning Source LLC
LaVergne TN
LVHW021739060526
838200LV00052B/3362